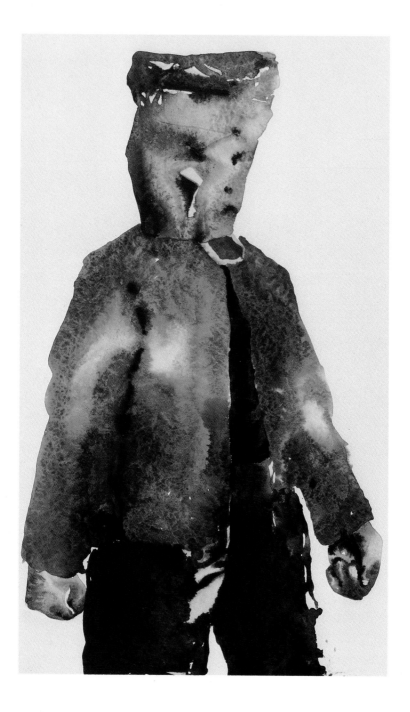

ROALD DAHL

Two Fables

WITH ILLUSTRATIONS BY

GRAHAM DEAN

FARRAR, STRAUS AND GIROUX

NEW YORK

Originally published in Great Britain by Viking, 1986
Published simultaneously in Canada by Collins Publishers, Toronto
Printed in the United States of America
First American edition, 1987
Designed by Bet Ayer

Library of Congress Cataloging-in-Publication Data
Dahl, Roald.
Two fables.
Contents: The Princess and the poacher—Princess Mammalia.
I. Dahl, Roald. Princess Mammalia. II. Title.
PR6054.A35T95   1987   823'.914   87-6

CONTENTS

THE

PRINCESS

AND THE

POACHER

Although Hengist was now eighteen years old, he still showed no desire to follow in his father's trade of basket-weaving. He even refused to go out and collect the osiers from the river-bank. This saddened his parents greatly, but they were wise enough to know that it seldom pays to force a young lad to work at something when his heart is not in it.

In appearance, Hengist was an exceedingly unattractive youth. With his squat body, his short bandy legs, his extra-long arms and his crumpled face, he looked almost as though there might be a touch of the ape or the gorilla about him. He was certainly mighty strong. He could bend double a two-inch-thick iron bar with his hands alone, and once he had astonished an old carter whose horse had fallen into a ditch by lifting the animal out bodily in his arms and placing it back on the road.

Quite naturally, Hengist was interested in maidens fair. But as one might expect, no maidens, fair or otherwise, were interested in Hengist. He was a pleasant enough fellow, there was no doubt about that, but there is a limit to the degree of ugliness any woman can tolerate in a man. Hengist was well beyond that limit. In fact, his ugliness was so extreme that no female other than his mother would have anything to do with him. This was a great sorrow to the lad. It was also grossly unfair, because no man is responsible for his own looks.

Poor Hengist. Although he knew that every maid and every wench in the kingdom was far beyond his reach for ever, he continued to long for them and lust after them with unabated passion. Whenever he spied a girl milking a cow or hanging out the washing, he would stop and stare and yearn most terribly to possess her.

Fortunately for him, he was soon to find another outlet for his energies. It had become a habit of his to take long walks in the countryside, through the forests and the glens, to cool his ardour, and over the ensuing weeks he began in some subtle way to fall in love with the landscape of the open air. He would spend his days roaming in deserted places, a silent, solitary, terribly uncouth figure, communing with nature. And thus, gradually and inevitably, he came to learn a great deal about the habits of animals and birds. He also discovered to his delight that he possessed the ability to move so silently through the forest that he could come within arm's length of a timid creature like a hare or a deer before it

was aware of his presence. This was not just from practice. It appeared to be a gift that had been bestowed upon him, a rare ability to merge into the landscape and suddenly to emerge again, almost like a ghost, when no man or bird or beast had seen him coming.

His family were very poor and they hardly ever tasted meat or game from one year to the next. Quite understandably, and quite soon, it dawned upon Hengist that he could very easily improve their lot, and indeed his own, by doing a little poaching. He began slowly, with a rabbit or a partridge once a week, but it was not long before the sheer pleasure and excitement of the chase took hold of him. Here, after all, was something he could do extraordinarily well. Poaching was an art. The thrill of creeping up on a crouching hare undetected or of snatching a roosting pheasant from a branch gave him a sense of satisfaction such as he had never known before. He became addicted to the sport.

But poaching was a hazardous occupation in the Kingdom. All the land, all the forests and the streams were owned either by the King himself or by one of the great Dukes, and although the footpaths on their estates were open to the public for strolling quietly, poaching on these lands was strictly forbidden. Anyone who strayed off the designated footpaths did so at his peril. The undergrowth was strewn with cunningly concealed man-traps whose iron jaws could bite a man's leg to the bone if he stepped on the plate that released the spring. And there the poor captive would remain, pinned to the ground, until a patrolling keeper found him the next day.

In the eyes of the King and the Dukes, poaching was a greater crime than murder. The sentence for murder was simply death by hanging, but the sentence for poaching was far more unpleasant. A convicted poacher would first be weighed on a special balance. Then two leaden anklets would be constructed whose weight had been most carefully calculated by the Royal Mathematician. These anklets would be fastened around the victim's ankles and his hands tied behind his back before he was lowered into the great Drowning Tub that was built of stone and stood permanently in the Market Square of the capital. The man's height had also been measured beforehand by the Mathematician, and a quantity of water had either been added to or taken out of the Tub so that when the man stood on tiptoe on the bottom, the top of his head was just below the surface of the water. The result of all this was that the victim spent many hours, sometimes days, being pulled down by the weight of the anklets, then jumping up again for a quick breath of air when his feet touched the bottom. Finally he sank altogether from exhaustion. The uncomfortable nature of this punishment did much to discourage the population

from breaking the law of the land. The hunting of game was the prerogative only of the Royal Family and the Dukes.

But Hengist was not to be intimidated. He had such faith in his powers of stealth that he harboured no fears of the dreaded Drowning Tub. His parents were, of course, frightened out of their skins. Every evening when he went out, and every dawn when he returned with a juicy partridge or a leveret under his coat, they trembled for their son, and indeed for themselves. But hunger is a powerful persuader and the spoils were always accepted and roasted and devoured with relish.

'You *are* being careful, son, are you not?' the mother would say, as she munched upon the tender breast of a woodcock.

'I is always careful, ma,' Hengist would answer. 'That little 'ole King and them fancy

Dooks they ain't never goin' to lay a finger on me.'

Hengist soon became so confident in his powers of poaching that he scorned the cover of darkness and took to going out in full daylight, which was something that only the bravest or the most foolhardy would do. And then one day, on a fine morning in springtime, he decided to have a go at the most protected area in the entire Kingdom, that part of the Royal Forest which lies immediately beneath the walls of the Castle itself, where the King lived. Here the game was more plentiful than anywhere else, but the dangers were tremendous. Hengist, as he crept soft and silent into the Royal Forest, was relishing this danger.

And now he was standing immobile in the shadow of a mighty beech, watching a young roebuck grazing not five paces away and waiting for the moment to pounce. Out of the edge of one eye he could see the south wall of the Royal Castle itself and somewhere in the distance he could hear bugles blowing. They were probably changing the guard at the gates, he told himself. Then suddenly, out of that same eye, he caught sight of a figure among the trees, not forty paces distant. Slowly, he turned his head to examine this person more carefully and, lo and behold, he saw immediately that it was none other than the young Princess, the only child of the King and the jewel in his crown. She was a young damsel of breathtaking beauty, with skin as pure and smooth as a silken glove, and she was but seventeen years old. Here she was then, apparently idling away the morning picking bluebells in the wood. Hengist's heart gave a jump when he saw her and all the old passions came flooding back once again. For a mad moment or two, he considered surprising the damsel by kneeling before her with whispered words of love and adoration, but he knew only too well what would happen then. She would take one look at his terrible ugliness and run away screaming, and he would be caught and put to death. It also occurred to him that he might creep upon her stealthily, coming up behind her unseen then clapping a hand over her mouth and having his way with her by force. But he quickly pushed this foul notion out of his mind, for he abhorred violence of any kind.

What happened next came very suddenly. There was a fanfare of hunting horns nearby and Hengist turned and saw a massive wild boar, the largest he had ever seen, come charging through the trees, and behind it, some fifty paces back, was riding the King himself and a group of noblemen, all galloping full-tilt after the boar

with lances drawn. The Princess was right in the
path of the running boar and the boar was in no
mood to swerve around her. Just the opposite.
An angry hunted boar will attack any human
who stands in its line of flight. Worse still, it will
often swing aside and attack an innocent by-
stander who might happen to be near. And
now the boar had spotted the Princess, and it was
making straight for her. Hengist saw the maiden
drop her bunch of bluebells and run. Then she
seemed to realize the futility of this, and she
stopped and pressed herself against the trunk
of a giant oak, and there she stood, helpless,
with arms outspread as though for crucifixion,
waiting for the madly rushing beast to reach
her. Hengist saw the boar, the size of a small
bull, charging forward with head down, the two
sharp, glistening tusks pointing straight at the
victim.

He took off like an arrow. He flew over the ground with his feet hardly touching the earth, and when he realized that the boar was going to reach the Princess before him, he made a last, despairing dive through the air and reached far out with his hands and just managed to grab hold of the boar's tusks when they were within a fraction of the maiden's midriff. Both Hengist and the boar went tumbling over in a heap, but the youth held on to the tusks, and when he leaped to his feet again, the boar came with him, lifted on high by the strongest pair of arms in the Kingdom. Hengist gave a sudden twist with his hands and even the King, some thirty paces distant, heard the boar's cervical spine snap in two. Hengist then swung the massive beast back and forth a couple of times before sending it sailing over his head as easily as if it had been a stick of fire-wood.

The King reached them first, galloping like mad and reining in his frothing horse right beside his daughter. He was followed by half a dozen noblemen, who all pulled up behind the King. The King leaped from his charger crying out, 'My darling! My little child! Are you all right?' He had witnessed the whole of the four-second drama, and in truth, when he had seen the boar charging straight for his daughter, he thought she was finished. And then he had seen this extraordinary human arrow leaping and flying between the trees and flinging himself upon the terrible boar just in the nick of time. The King was white in the face as he took the sobbing Princess in his arms to console her. Hengist stood awkwardly by, not quite knowing what to do with his hands or his feet or anything else.

At last the King turned to look at Hengist. For a moment or two, the shock of seeing such a

spectacularly ugly youth rendered him speech-
less. But he kept on looking, and as he looked, he
found himself liking more and more what he
saw. A man is seldom repelled by the malformed
features of another man. Quite the reverse. Men,
as a whole, take less kindly to other men who are
exceptionally good-looking. Women are often
the same with other women. Yet, as we all know,
good looks do have a profound influence upon
the *opposite* sex. This is a fact of life, but as the
wise King knew, it caused much disillusionment
later on. Yes, the King was telling himself, as he
continued to stare at this curious fellow who
stood before him, how different he is from the
sloppy, effeminate, lecherous young courtiers
who surround me at the Castle! This is a real man!
He is brave and swift and fearless, and to hell
with his looks! It was at this point that a sly plot
began to hatch in the King's devious mind.

In his rich royal voice, charged with emotion, he said, 'Young man, today you have done me the greatest service any citizen could perform for his King! You have saved the treasure of my life, the pearl of my Kingdom, my only child, indeed the only child I shall ever have because the poor Queen is dead! I intend to see that you are rewarded in a munificent manner! Pray accompany me to the Castle at once!'

Then the King lifted the Princess up on to his charger and himself got into the saddle behind her. The entourage rode off at a trot, with a rather bemused Hengist running alongside.

As soon as he arrived at the Castle, the King summoned a meeting of the Elders. Ostensibly, these old men were the parliament that ruled the Kingdom, but in reality it was the King himself who decided everything. No man dared gainsay the monarch.

In the Council Chamber the Elder

wenty in all, were assembled in their pews.

Above, on a dais, sat the King upon his throne, and beside him stood Hengist. The latter was not very suitably attired for the occasion. He wore a shirt made from some kind of sacking, his breeches were filthy, and on his stockingless feet was a pair of home-made sandals. The Elders stared at this ugly, ill-dressed creature with distaste. The King smiled. He was a curious man, the King, much given to eccentricities and japes and ingenious practical jokes. For example, at his dining-table, which seated twelve guests, he had twelve little taps concealed under the edge of the table, and if any of his guests, male or female, annoyed him or said something foolish, the King would reach under the table and open the appropriate tap. This would send a powerful jet of water from a tiny hole in the centre of the chair right up the backside of the offending guest.

It had not taken the King long to realize that
Hengist, with those terribly ugly features, must
be the most sexually disappointed man in the
Kingdom. He had actually observed several

31

ladies of the court recoiling and covering their faces as the youth passed by. All this suited his subtle plan very well.

'Learned Elders,' he said, addressing the Council, 'this gallant youth, Hengist by name, has by an act of unbelievable bravery saved the life of the Princess, your future Queen. No reward is too great for him. He shall therefore be granted a stipend of one thousand gold crowns a year and shall be accommodated in a grace-and-favour mansion on the Royal Estate. He shall be provided with servants and a lavish wardrobe and whatever else he desires for his comfort.'

'Hear hear,' the Elders murmured. 'He well deserves it.'

'But that is a mere nothing compared to what other favours I am now about to grant him,' the King went on. 'I have decided that the greatest reward I can bestow upon this valiant and gallant youth is as follows. By Royal Decree, he shall also be granted . . .' Here the King paused dramatically. The Elders waited. 'He shall be granted the absolute right to ravish any maiden, wench, lady, dame, Countess, Duchess or other female in the Kingdom whenever he so desires.'

There was uproar among the Elders. 'You can't do that!' they cried. 'What about our wives? What about our daughters?'

'What about them?' the King asked. 'You will notice that I have not even excluded the Princess, so why should I exclude your wretched wives or daughters?'

'You mustn't do this, Your Majesty!' the Elders cried out. 'There will be chaos at court! There will be rape in the corridors! The whole place will be bedlam! Our poor innocent daughters! Our dear wives!'

'I doubt your daughters or wives will qualify,'

the King remarked drily. 'Only great beauties will stand a chance of being noticed. When a man has his pick, he chooses carefully.'

'We beg you, Majesty!' the Elders cried. 'Do not force us to pass such a law!'

'Nothing you say will deter me,' said the King. 'And, furthermore, I decree that any lady who refuses to submit to the blandishments of Count Hengist – I have just made him a Count, by the way – will be put to death in the Drowning Tub.'

The Elders were all on their feet waving their order papers and shouting against the King. 'You've gone too far!' they cried. 'There will be sexual anarchy in the land!'

'Don't be so sure,' said the clever King.

'Sexual anarchy!' the Elders chanted. 'Rape on the ramparts! It's not good enough!'

'Listen,' said the King, beginning to lose patience. 'I'll have the whole lot of you put in the

Drowning Tub if you give me any more trouble!'

That shut them up.

'Lastly,' the King continued, 'and you'd better note this carefully, any man, any father or husband or brother, who attempts to interfere with the noble Count in the pursuance of his desires shall also be put in the Drowning Tub. Do I make myself clear?' There was a steely edge to the King's voice, and the Elders sat down and remained silent and sulked. They knew that their ruler, who had the entire army behind him to a man, was all-powerful. He always got his way.

'Draw up the Proclamation immediately,' the King said. 'Have it posted in towns and villages all over the Kingdom. Have the town-criers call out the news in every hamlet! Tell the population that Count Hengist enjoys the freedom of all the women in the realm. And be sure to stress the penalties for disobedience. See also that Count

Hengist himself be given a Card of Authority
that he can wave in the face of any
maiden or wench he may desire.'

Thus, this extraordinary Decree was made law,
and Hengist, under the full protection of the
King, moved into a mansion near the Castle
where servants bathed him and groomed him
and taught him how to dress in the style of the
court.

At first, the poor fellow was totally bewildered. He wandered awkwardly about the court, shunned by everybody. The Dukes snubbed him or ignored him. The ladies ran for their lives whenever he hove in sight. And who could blame them? Not even the most lascivious courtesans wanted to go near the poor fellow. He was treated by one and all as though he had leprosy.

But a strange thing had happened to Hengist. His desires seemed suddenly to have evaporated. He knew all about the immense powers he possessed. He was aware that he had the full backing of the King. He could seek out and ravish any maiden he desired, not only at court, but in the towns and villages all over the country. The trouble was, he did not desire them. He felt no urge at all. It was the old story of the forbidden fruit. Make it easy to get and the appetite goes away.

The King, who had been watching all this for several weeks with wry amusement, was strolling one morning on the ramparts with the Princess when suddenly Hengist happened by. 'How goes it, my lad?' said the King, slapping the youth on the back.

'Your Majesty,' Hengist said, 'to tell the truth, I doesn't much care for this thing you 'as done to me.'

'My dear chap,' said the King, 'what on earth is the trouble?'

'Nobody likes me around 'ere,' Hengist said. 'They is all treatin' me like dirt.'

'*I* like you,' said the Princess suddenly.

Hengist stared at her. 'You does?' he said.

'You are the only man in the Castle who does not chase me along the corridors,' the Princess said. 'You are the only decent person in the whole place.'

'Now I come to think of it, my darling,' said the King, smiling a little, 'I suppose you're right.'

'I know I'm right, daddy,' the young beauty said. 'All the other men around here are totally disgusting. I hate them.'

'Some of them are very handsome, my dear,' the King said.

'That's got nothing to do with it!' cried the Princess. 'I don't give a fig about looks!'

'You mean you likes me a little bit?' Hengist inquired nervously.

'*Like you?*' cried the Princess, flinging herself into his arms. 'I love you!'

The King slipped away, leaving them alone. He was well pleased with the way things had worked out.

PRINCESS
MAMMALIA

hen Princess Mammalia arose from her bed on the morning of her seventeenth birthday and examined her face in the looking-glass, she couldn't believe what she saw. Up until then she had always been a rather plain and dumpy girl with a thick neck, but now she suddenly found herself staring at a young lady she had never set eyes on before. A magical transformation had taken place overnight and the dumpy little Princess had become a dazzling beauty. I use the word 'dazzling' in its purest and most literal sense, for such a blaze of glory, such a scintillation of stars, such a blinding beauty shone forth from her countenance that when she went down-stairs an hour later to open her presents, those who gazed upon her at close quarters had to screw up their eyes for fear the brilliance of it all might damage their retinas. Even the royal astronomer was heard to murmur that it might be safer to view the lady through smoked glass, as one would the eclipse of the sun.

Ever since she had learned to walk, Princess Mammalia had been much loved around the Palace for her modest and gentle disposition, but she very soon found out that it is much more difficult for a ravishing beauty to remain modest and gentle than it is for a plain girl. She discovered that the kind of extraordinary beauty she possessed endowed her with immense power. In the glittering presence of her new-found image, men became so overwhelmed with desire that they were hers to command. Caliphs and rajas, grand viziers and generals,

47

48

ministers and chancellors, camel drivers and rent collectors, all of them melted into a froth as soon as she appeared on the scene. They fawned and simpered. They drooled and dribbled. They crawled and toadied. She had only to lift her little finger and they all started scampering around the room in their efforts to please her. They offered her rich jewels and golden bracelets. They suggested lavish feasts in cool places, and whenever one of them got her in a corner on her own, he began to whisper obscenities in her ear. There were also problems with the staff. A servant is just as much of a man as a courtier, and after several unsavoury incidents in the corridors, the King was forced, much against his wishes, for he was a kind King, to order that all male servants in the Palace be castrated immediately. Only the royal chef escaped. He pleaded that it would ruin his cooking.

At first, and with charming innocence, the Princess simply sat back and enjoyed her new-found power. But that couldn't go on. Nobody, let alone a maiden of seventeen, could remain unaffected for long. This was power indeed. It was power unheard of in one so young. And power itself, the Princess soon discovered, is a demanding taskmaster. It is impossible to have it and not use it. It insists on being exercised. Thus the Princess began consciously to exercise her power over men, first in small ways, then in rather bigger ones. It was ridiculously easy, like manipulating puppets.

At this point, the Princess made her second discovery, and it was this. If the power of a female is so great that men will obey her without question, she becomes contemptuous of those men, and within a month, the Princess found that the only feelings she had towards the male species were those of scorn and contumely. She began to practise all manner of droll strategems to humiliate her worshippers. She took, for example, to going on walkabouts in the city and displaying herself to ordinary men in the street. Surrounded by her faithful guard of eunuchs, she would watch with amusement as the male citizens went crazy with desire at the sight of her blazing beauty, hurling themselves against the spears of the guards and becoming impaled by the hundreds.

51

Late at night, before retiring to bed, she would divert herself by strolling out on to her balcony and showing herself to the lascivious *polloi* who were wont to gather in their thousands in the courtyard below, hoping for a glimpse of her. And why not indeed? She looked more dazzling and desirable than ever standing there in the moonlight. In truth, she outshone the moon itself, and the citizens would go berserk as soon as she appeared, crying out and tearing their hair and fracturing their bones by flinging themselves against the craggy walls of the Palace. Every now and again, the Princess would pour a pipkin or two of boiling lead over their heads to cool them down.

All this was bad enough, but there was worse to come. As we all know, power, with all its subtle facets, is a voracious bedfellow. The more one has, the more one wants. There is no such thing as getting enough of it, and over the next few months the Princess's craving for power grew and grew until in the end she found herself beginning to toy with the idea of gaining for herself the ultimate power in the land, the throne itself.

She was the eldest of seven children, all of them girls, and her mother was dead. Already, therefore, she was the rightful heir to her father's throne. But what good was that? Her father, the King, who not so long ago had been the idol of her eye, now irritated her to distraction. He was a benign and merciful ruler, much loved by his people, and because he was her father he was the only man in the Kingdom who did not turn cartwheels at the sight of her. What was worse, he was in excellent health.

Such is the terrible corrupting influence of power that the young Princess now began actually to plot the destruction of her own father. But that was easier said than done. It is extremely difficult to bump off a great ruler all on your own

without being caught. Poison was a possibility, but poisoners are nearly always apprehended. She spent many days and nights ruminating upon this problem, but no answer came to her. Then one evening after supper, she strolled out on to her balcony as usual, thinking to divert herself for a few moments by driving the crowd of lecherous citizens crazy but, lo and behold, on this night there was no crowd. Instead, an old beggerman stood alone in the courtyard, gazing up at her. He was dressed in filthy rags and his feet were bare. He had a long white beard and a mane of snow-white hair that reached to his shoulders, and he leaned heavily upon a stick. "Go away, you disgusting old man,' she called out.

'Ssshh!' the old beggar whispered, edging closer. 'I am here to help you. It has come to me in a vision that you are deeply troubled.'

'I am not in the least troubled,' the Princess answered. 'Be off with you unless you fancy a pipkin of boiling lead over your noddle.'

The old man ignored her. 'There is only one way in the world,' he whispered, 'to dispose of an enemy without being caught. Do you wish to hear it?'

'Certainly not,' the Princess snapped. 'Why should I? Yes, what is it?'

'You take an oyster,' the old man whispered, 'and you bury it in the soil of a potted plant. Twenty-four hours later, you dig it up and you squeeze one droplet of its juice, just one droplet, mind you, on to each of the oysters that you are serving to the victim on the following day.'

'Does that fix him?' the Princess asked, unable to conceal her interest.

'It is lethal,' whispered the old man. 'The person who eats those oysters will succumb very swiftly to a terrible paroxysm that will tie his whole body into knots. And after it is over, the whole world will simply shake their heads and murmur, "Poor fellow, he ate a very bad oyster." '

'Who are you, old man, and where do you come from?' the Princess asked, leaning over the balcony.

'I am on the side of the righteous,' the old man whispered, and with that he disappeared into the shadows.

The Princess stored this information away in her head and patiently bided her time. A few days before her eighteenth birthday, the King said to her, 'What do you want for your birthday dinner, my dear? Shall it be your favourite roast boar as usual?'

'Yes, papa,' she answered. 'But let us have some oysters first. I do so love oysters.'

'What a capital idea,' answered the King. 'I shall send to the coast for them immediately.'

On the Princess's birthday, the table in the great dining-room was sumptuously laid and all was got ready for the feast. One dozen fine oysters were put in each place, but before the guests went in to take their seats, the King entered the room alone, as was his wont on special occasions, to make sure that all was to his liking. He summoned the butler and together the two of them walked slowly round the table.

'Why,' asked the King, pointing to his own plate, 'have you given to me the biggest and choicest oysters?'

'Your Majesty always receives the best of

everything,' replied the butler, speaking in a high voice. 'Have I done wrong?'

'Today the Princess Mammalia must have the best,' the King said. 'She is the birthday girl. So kindly give her my plate and give me hers.'

'At once, Your Majesty,' answered the butler, and he hastened to change the plates round.

The birthday feast was a success and the oysters went down particularly well. 'Do you like them, papa?' Princess Mammalia kept asking her father. 'Are they not succulent?'

'Mine are delicious,' the King said. 'How are yours?'

'Perfect,' she answered. 'They are just perfect.'

That night Princess Mammalia was taken violently ill, and despite the ministrations of the royal physician, she succumbed to a terrible paroxysm that tied her beautiful body into knots.